MEET the MINI-MAMMALS
A Night at the Natural History Museum

Written by
Melissa Stewart

Illustrated by
Brian Lies

Beach Lane Books
New York   London   Toronto   Sydney   New Delhi

You probably already know a lot about **BIG** mammals like elephants and hippos and giraffes.

That's why *this* exhibit celebrates small.

WHAT'S A MAMMAL?

You're a mammal. So are cats, dogs, hippos, giraffes, dolphins, elephants, and all the mini-mammals in this book. A mammal can make heat to keep its body warm. It has a backbone and at least a little bit of hair. A mama mammal feeds her young milk that she makes in her body.

Get ready to meet some of the world's most amazing mini-mammals. See them at their actual size and find out which has the teeny-tiniest body of all.

Hello, Japanese dwarf flying squirrel!

This little critter spends its nights dashing through the treetops in search of seeds, buds, bark, and fruit. If it senses danger, it jumps for its life. Thanks to skin flaps that stretch from its wrists to its ankles, the flying squirrel gracefully glides to safety. Even though this mini-mammal is small enough to hold in your hand, it can travel the length of eight school buses with one leap.

Tiny Tidbit: A Japanese dwarf flying squirrel weighs about the same as a small Asian pear.

Is *this* lively leaper the mini-est mammal of all?

No! Hello, southern lesser galago!

ACTUAL SIZE!

A moth is no match for this petite predator. A galago can easily snatch insects out of the air with its front feet. Between snacks, it scampers through the forest, hopping from tree to tree. It sprays its feet with sticky urine to help it grip branches. After a night of hunting alone, a galago finds its family. The group grooms one another. Then they fall asleep in a huddled heap.

Tiny Tidbit: A southern lesser galago weighs about the same as a softball.

Is *this* fluffy furball the mini-est mammal of all?

No! Hello, lesser hedgehog tenrec!

ACTUAL SIZE!

During the day, this prickly peewee rests under a rotting log. At night, it wanders across the ground, sniffing its surroundings. If it catches the scent of an insect, it attacks. It also hunts small lizards and baby mice. When the teeny tenrec feels scared, it rolls into a ball. Watch out! It might lunge backward and try to stab you with its sharp spines.

Tiny Tidbit: A lesser hedgehog tenrec weighs about the same as a softball.

Is *this* itty-bitty beast the mini-est mammal of all?

Hey, mischievous munchkins,
what are you doing here?
Get back to your spots!

Hello, Philippine tarsier!

ACTUAL SIZE!

My, what big eyes a tarsier has! They're perfect for spotting insects, frogs, lizards, and bats—even on the darkest nights. As this mini-mammal munches its meal, it presses its long tail against a tree trunk for support. Sticky pads on its long toes help it cling to the bark. After a night of feeding, the tiny tarsier scouts out a tree hole near the ground. It climbs inside, curls into a ball, and drifts off to sleep.

Tiny Tidbit: A Philippine tarsier weights about the same as a stick of butter.

Is *this* tiny tree dweller the mini-est mammal of all?

No! Hello, least chipmunk!

As summer ends, this striped sprinter gets ready for cold, snowy weather. It stuffs its chubby cheeks with nuts and seeds. Then it heads back to its burrow. In winter, the chipmunk snoozes for a few days at a time. Between naps, it nibbles on its supply of snacks. And when warm days return, it shakes itself awake and springs into action.

Tiny Tidbit: A least chipmunk weighs about the same as a golf ball.

Is *this* nimble nibbler the mini-est mammal of all?

No! Hello, Madame Berthe's mouse lemur!

ACTUAL SIZE!

In warm, wet weather, this quick critter spends its nights bounding along branches. It gorges on fruits, flowers, and tree sap. It gobbles insects, spiders, and small lizards too. During the cool, dry season, these foods are hard to find, so the mouse lemur changes its diet to . . . insect poop. But the watery waste doesn't provide all the energy it needs. To survive, the wee one lowers its body temperature and slows its breathing while it sleeps.

Tiny Tidbit: A Madame Berthe's mouse lemur weighs about the same as a crayon.

Is *this* palm-sized pipsqueak the mini-est mammal of all?

Hey, rambunctious rascals, what are you doing here? Get back to your spots!

Hello, American shrew mole!

ACTUAL SIZE!

This mini-mole may be the world's strangest sleeper. It dozes for about eight minutes at a time, then hunts for up to eighteen minutes before it needs another nap. To find earthworms, slugs, and centipedes, it tap-tap-taps its nose in the dirt. Then it takes a step forward and taps some more. When it finally touches its target . . . *Chomp!*

Tiny Tidbit: An American shrew mole weighs about the same as two raspberries.

Is *this* tiny tyke the mini-est mammal of al

No! Hello, dwarf three-toed jerboa!

During the day, this mini-mammal sleeps in an underground den. At night, it hop-hop-hops across the desert. When it finds tasty seeds or leaves, it grabs the food with its front feet and chows down. It gets all the water it needs by nibbling on roots.

Tiny Tidbit: A dwarf three-toed jerboa weighs about the same as two tea bags.

Is *this* pinky-sized peewee the mini-est mammal of all?

No! Hello, Etruscan pygmy shrew!

What's this small shrew's claim to fame? It lives its life at top speed. Its heart beats fifteen times faster than yours. And it takes forty breaths in the time you take just one. To keep its body running, the hungry hunter eats twice its weight in food every single night. That's like a ten-year-old kid devouring more than five hundred hamburgers a day.

Tiny Tidbit: An Etruscan pygmy shrew weighs about the same as three mini marshmallows.

Is *this* speedy snacker the mini-est mammal of all?

Aha, there you are.
Get back to your spot!

Hello, Kitti's hog-nosed bat!

This itty-bitty bat spends most of its time hanging upside down deep inside a cave. At dusk, it hunts insects and spiders for just thirty minutes. Then it heads home. At dawn, it spends about twenty more minutes foraging for food.

Tiny Tidbit: A Kitti's hog-nosed bat weighs a little less than four mini marshmallows.

Is *this* furry flier the mini-est mammal

Why, yes, it is! Just look at that teeny-tiny body.

4. American shrew mole
6. Least chipmunk

Three cheers for the mini-mammals! Let's give them all a hand.

Mini-Mammal Small Stats

10. Japanese dwarf flying squirrel

Scientific name: *Pteromys momonga*
Habitat: Forest
Body length: 6.5 in (16.5 cm)
Tail length: 5 in (12.7 cm)
Weight: 6.5 oz (184 g)
Life span: 5 years
Curator's note: When a flying squirrel pup is born, it has no fur. You can see its heart, lungs, and stomach through its skin.

8. Lesser hedgehog tenrec

Scientific name: *Echinops telfairi*
Habitat: Forest, grassland, scrubland
Body length: 6 in (15.3 cm)
Tail length: 0.5 in (1.3 cm)
Weight: 7 oz (198 g)
Life span: 9 years
Curator's note: As a tenrec climbs a tree, it can hang from a branch by one toe.

6. Least chipmunk

Scientific name: *Neotamias minimus*
Habitat: Forest, rocky cliffs, scrubland
Body length: 4 in (10.2 cm)
Tail length: 4 in (10.2 cm)
Weight: 1.7 oz (48 g)
Life span: Up to 6 years
Curator's note: Twenty-four kinds of chipmunks live in North America. This one is the smallest.

9. Southern lesser galago

Scientific name: *Galago moholi*
Habitat: Forest; dry, grassy woodland
Body length: 6.3 in (16 cm)
Tail length: 7.5 in (19 cm)
Weight: 7 oz (198 g)
Life span: 15 years
Curator's note: Some people call galagoes "bush babies" because their calls sound like a human baby crying.

7. Philippine tarsier

Scientific name: *Carlito syrichta*
Habitat: Tropical rainforest
Body length: 4.5 in (11.4 cm)
Tail length: 9 in (22.9 cm)
Weight: 4 oz (113 g)
Life span: 13 years
Curator's note: A tarsier is always on the lookout for danger. Like an owl, it can twist its head to see what's behind it.

5. Madame Berthe's mouse lemur

Scientific name: *Microcebus berthae*
Habitat: Forest
Body length: 3.5 in (8.9 cm)
Tail length: 5 in (12.7 cm)
Weight: 1.1 oz (31 g)
Life span: 5 years
Curator's note: When the Madame Berthe's mouse lemur was discovered in 1992, there were only two known species of mouse lemurs. Today there are twenty-four!

For Gerard, who inspired this book —M. S.

In memory of Terry Shay— friend, beloved teacher, and passionate advocate for reading and children's literature. —B. L.

BEACH LANE BOOKS • An imprint of Simon & Schuster Children's Publishing Division • 1230 Avenue of the Americas, New York, New York 10020 • Text © 2025 by Melissa Stewart • Illustration © 2025 by Brian Lies • Book design by Lauren Rille • All rights reserved, including the right of reproduction in whole or in part in any form. BEACH LANE BOOKS and colophon are trademarks of Simon & Schuster, LLC. • For information about special discounts for bulk purchases, please contact Simon & Schuster Special Sales at 1-866-506-1949 or business@simonandschuster.com. • The Simon & Schuster Speakers Bureau can bring authors to your live event. For more information or to book an event, contact the Simon & Schuster Speakers Bureau at 1-866-248-3049 or visit our website at www.simonspeakers.com. • The text for this book was set in Oxtail. • The illustrations for this book were rendered in acrylic paint and colored pencil on Strathmore paper. • Manufactured in China • 1024 SCP • First Edition
10 9 8 7 6 5 4 3 2 1
Library of Congress Cataloging-in-Publication Data • Names: Stewart, Melissa, author. | Lies, Brian, illustrator. • Title: Meet the mini-mammals / Melissa Stewart ; illustrated by Brian Lies. • Description: First edition. | New York : Beach Lane Books, [2025] | Includes bibliographical references. | Audience: Ages 4–8 | Audience: Grades 2-3 | Summary: "Meet some of the world's very smallest mini-mammals, and see them at their actual size, in this adorable and informative nonfiction picture book"—Provided by publisher. Identifiers: LCCN 2024005675 (print) | LCCN 2024005676 (ebook) | ISBN 9781665947169 (hardcover) | ISBN 9781665947176 (ebook) • Subjects: LCSH: Mammals—Juvenile literature. | Body size—Juvenile literature. | Classification: LCC QL706.2 .S753 2025 (print) | LCC QL706.2 (ebook) | DDC 599—dc23/eng/20240419 • LC record available at https://lccn.loc.gov/2024005675 • LC ebook record available at https://lccn.loc.gov/2024005676

3 · Dwarf three-toed jerboa

Scientific name: *Salpingotulus michaelis*

Habitat: Desert

Body length: 1.7 in (4.3 cm)

Tail length: 3 in (7.6 cm)

Weight: 0.13 oz (3.7 g)

Life span: 2 years

Curator's note: A dwarf three-toed jerboa's back feet are four times longer than its front feet. It can jump more than 9 ft (3 m).

1 · Kitti's hog-nosed bat

Scientific name: *Craseonycteris thonglongyai*

Habitat: Forest, limestone cave

Body length: 1.3 in (3.3 cm)

Wingspan: 6.5 in (16.5 cm)

Weight: 0.07 oz (2 g)

Life span: Up to 10 years

Curator's note: Many people call this little critter the "bumblebee bat" because it's about the same size as the buzzy insect.

4 · American shrew mole

Scientific name: *Neurotrichus gibbsii*

Habitat: Forest, swamp

Body length: 3 in (7.6 cm)

Tail length: 1 in (2.5 cm)

Weight: 0.35 oz (9.9 g)

Life span: 1 year

Curator's note: An American shrew mole may eat as much as 50 lbs (23 kg) of earthworms in a year.

2 · Etruscan pygmy shrew

Scientific name: *Suncus etruscus*

Habitat: Forest, scrubland, grassland

Body length: 1.5 in (3.8 cm)

Tail length: 1 in (2.5 cm)

Weight: 0.06 oz (1.8 g)

Life span: 1.5 years

Curator's note: An Etruscan pygmy shrew can catch prey almost as big as it is, including froglets, young lizards, and newborn mice.

Selected Sources

Animal Diversity Web, http://animaldiversity.org.

Clutton-Brock, Juliet and Don E. Wilson. *Smithsonian Handbooks: Mammals.* New York: Dorling Kindersley Limited, 2002.

Gursky-Doyen, Sharon. "Married to the Mob." *Natural History,* October 2010, 20–26.

* Lunde, Darrin. *Hello, Bumblebee Bat.* Watertown, MA: Charlesbridge, 2007.

* Morris, Pat and Amy-Jane Beer. *The World of Animals: Mammals,* vols. 1, 7, 8, 9, 10. Danbury, CT: Grolier, 2003.

Oosthuizen, Noelle. "Bushbabies: The Southern Lesser Galagoes." *Africa Geographic Stories,* August 16, 2019. https://magazine.africageographic.com/weekly/issue-268/bushbabies-southern-lesser-galago/.

* San Diego Zoo Wildlife Alliance: Animals & Plants, https://animals.sandiegozoo.org/animals.

* Smithsonian's National Zoo & Conservation Biology Institute, https://nationalzoo.si.edu/animals.

* Wendell, Bryan. "It's a Small World: The Big Story Behind Some of Earth's Tiniest Animals." *Boys Life.* October 1, 2015, 8.

* Recommended for curious kids.